The Trilogy of Uncertainty

Matthew Lotti

ISBN-10: 0-9715594-7-3
ISBN-13: 978-0-9715594-7-9

"It is so difficult to find the beginning. Or, better: it is difficult to begin at the beginning. And not try to go further back."

- Ludwig Wittgenstein

Contents

Battles We Have Fought and Won 7

The Cut-Paper Shadow 36

Silver Light, Good Morning 62

Battles We Have Fought and Won

A Play in One Act

2010

CHARACTERS

Angoilino, a firefighter in his late 50's, early 60's. Physically imposing and has an air of authority about him.

Tommy, a firefighter in his mid-twenties. Lean but strong. His head is shaved.

* Both characters are to be wearing their regulation work uniforms, which consist of dark blue pants, dark blue short-sleeve shirts, black leather belts and black, polished boots. The left sleeves of their shirts have the fire emblem patches on them while the right sleeves have the American flag patches. The shirts have two buttoned pockets on the front, and above the left pockets are silver fire department badges.

Place: Outside a fire station.

Time: An autumn afternoon.

(*It's an autumn day outside of the local fire station. There are a precious few scattered leaves - red and orange - on the stage. There is a single deck chair, slightly off center. Tommy is sitting there, smoking a cigarette - the pack is in his shirt pocket - and staring at the ground, thinking.*

Tommy takes several seconds to collect himself. He stands up, paces slowly stage left, moves a few leaves around carefully with his boot, as if he's rearranging them in a precise way, shakes his head, then returns to the chair.

In a few moments, Angoilino comes out with a clear plastic bag of acorns in one hand and a lawn chair in the other. He sets the bag of acorns down and sets up the chair. He sits down.

Angoilino looks long and hard at Tommy.)

ANGOILINO: I hope you don't mind I have a seat.

TOMMY: Go ahead.

ANGOILINO: Good. (*Angoilino is still looking at Tommy. Tommy is still smoking and looking down.*) How many you up to?

TOMMY: Hmmm?

ANGOILINO: Your habit.

TOMMY: (*Thinking.*) It depends.

ANGOILINO: It depends on what.

TOMMY: The day.

ANGOILINO: At one point I was up to three packs a day. They were fifty cents at the time. My wife, well, we were dating then, she was working at a drugstore. And damaged packs were a quarter. So she used to step on them.

TOMMY: Fifty cents?

ANGOILINO: In the 70's. What're they up to? Now? 6 bucks? 7?

TOMMY: Something like that.

ANGOILINO: I quit when my wife got pregnant with my son. Cold turkey. No patches, no gum.

TOMMY: My C.O. started me on 'em. He told me it was good for my lungs.

ANGOILINO: (*Laughs.*) Right.

TOMMY: When people were e-mailing me and asking me what I wanted shipped to me over there, that was the first thing I wanted in my CARE package. That and talcum powder.

ANGOILINO: Sure.

TOMMY: My Uncle sent me cigars, too. Those were nice.

(*Angoilino gets up and opens up his bag of acorns and starts spreading a few of them along the ground. Tommy watches him but doesn't comment. Angoilino leaves about half the*

*acorns in the bag and sets it down next to the chair. He then
sits down.*)

ANGOILINO: There was a call for Seven so we're on stand-
by.

TOMMY: What for?

ANGOILINO: House. Last week, Gene and I went on a call
where the whole kitchen was gone. It was a mess. Old broad
that lived there didn't think the candle smelled good enough
so she sprayed perfume on it before she lit it. (*Pause.*) Went
upstairs to watch TV, smelled smoke. If she'd have fallen
asleep, she'd have been dead because the kitchen's below her
bedroom.

TOMMY: Perfume on a candle?

ANGOILINO: Perfume on a candle.

TOMMY: I like the guy who used an outdoor grill in his
bathroom. He didn't even realize he was doing anything
wrong.

ANGOILINO: When I took it out of there and threw it on
the lawn, he said I was burning his grass.

TOMMY: (*Shaking his head.*) Jesus. (*Pause.*) You filed
that report, right?

ANGOILINO: Last week.

TOMMY: I still laugh whenever I think about when that
fraternity dismantled their detectors and then that one guy—

ANGOILINO: (*Interrupting.*) They didn't dismantle them. They put Styrofoam over them.

TOMMY: Right, right, and then they made the excuse that they were going off in the middle of the night.

ANGOILINO: Then they didn't know how the bed ended up on fire.

TOMMY: It was probably some prankster.

ANGOILINO: Well, you weren't here, this was about ... six years ago or so, when we had to go to the same college this time it was in a dorm room. The kids were dipping rolls of toilet paper in alcohol, lighting them and bowling.

TOMMY: You didn't tell me this one.

ANGOILINO: No one admitted to doing it, everyone was saying they just got there, they didn't know what was happening ... then the Dean showed up and saw the tracks along the hallway and along the edges of the walls. (*Tommy laughs.*) She was *pissed.* When the school said the parents had to pay for the damages, the parents had a shit-fit and the kids started ratting each other out.

TOMMY: Anybody get expelled?

ANGOILINO: I have no idea. They don't tell us things like that.

TOMMY: We aren't detectives.

ANGOILINO: That we aren't. (*Long Pause.*) So why didn't you clean the truck when Richie asked you to?

TOMMY: (*Taken aback.*) I was supposed to do that?

ANGOILINO: Richie asked you Friday. Then I asked you Friday.

TOMMY: That's Jimmy's job.

ANGOILINO: That's your job.

TOMMY: But we take turns, right? Jimmy does it, then I do it.

(*Tommy gets up and moves towards stage right slowly. He lights another cigarette.*)

ANGOILINO: You were told to do it.

(*Tommy doesn't respond.*)

ANGOILINO: And I asked you to cut the grass on Monday. That's grass cutting day.

TOMMY: They said because of the drought...

ANGOILINO: *I* asked you to cut the grass. Didn't I? Didn't I tell you when you were inside that—

TOMMY: (*Interrupting.*) I heard you, I just didn't—

(*Angoilino stands up.*)

ANGOILINO: (*Interrupting.*) No, you didn't hear me, because you were eating and playing on your phone when I was talking to you. And you said "yeah" but it wasn't "yeah, I'm going to do that," it was "yeah, now shut up."

TOMMY: I wouldn't ever, I wouldn't tell you—

ANGOILINO: I have to keep sticking up for you with Richie. The truck ... who cares about the truck. I got a whole list. We were flushing hydrants in August, and you took off sick—

TOMMY: (*Interrupting.*) But I *was* sick.

ANGOILINO: I'm not saying you weren't, but you think I always feel good? You think I'm always here 100 percent? It's so many things. You turn down overtime, which is fine, but we could use you. You've been late a few times.

TOMMY: When was I late?

ANGOILINO: Richie says six times. And that you left early four times.

TOMMY: (*Stunned.*) He gave me permission *each and every one* of those times.

ANGOILINO: You still left early. And when you yelled at that old woman from 3rd Street—

TOMMY: (*Interrupting.*) She had that coming.

ANGOILINO: She did have it coming. But you can't say anything back. And who got time off for it? You did. You know how many people I want to scream at for being stupid? I either don't respond or say "We'll see what we can do." Half these people want to trap you and then they report you.

Should she have yelled at you? No. What was her exact problem? I don't know and neither do you. But you handled it wrong.

(*Tommy stops talking, starts pacing so slightly and steps on/kicks aside one of the acorns on the ground.*)

TOMMY: What's with the acorns?

ANGOILINO: They're for the squirrels. I got them from the backyard of my house.

TOMMY: You like squirrels that much?

ANGOILINO: I like owls. There's one in the tree over there that I listen for.

TOMMY: (*Nods.*) I think I've heard him before. (*Pause.*) I, I'm just ... I don't know that this job is right for me.

ANGOILINO: Well ... (*Goes to sit down.*) you have to think: what else should you do?

TOMMY: I don't know the answer to that.

ANGOILINO: Why come here in the first place? The first year is tough, you're at least off your probation period.

TOMMY: Everybody gets through probation.

ANGOILINO: That's because nobody wants to look stupid for hiring you.

TOMMY: Makes sense.

ANGOILINO: And you have your military points.

TOMMY: That is also true.

ANGOILINO: Those moved you right up the list.

TOMMY: I agree, I agree. (*Pause.*) I really like the job. I didn't want to be a cop. Met too many idiot MPs, never cared to do that. Didn't want a desk job. I like the whole, you know, we're here to help people. It's important. The new EMT and HAZMAT things we're doing are interesting.

ANGOILINO: (*Rolls head back in disgust.*) I hate that.

TOMMY: I know you do, and so does everyone else, and it's really more for paramedics, but it makes me feel well-rounded. It's because you guys got your job description changed. You got set in your ways. A buddy of mine's always joking with me, talking about "Didja get any cats out of the tree today?" because people think we do that. "Sell any smoke detectors? Get cats out of trees?" I think this is what people think we do.

ANGOILINO: So you say you like the job. That's a good beginning. You're not like my kid, who's working in insurance and wants to hang himself because he's locked inside all day. You made a decision. So how come you can't get your head out of your ass? How come you're jerking around? Why am I sick of the front office complaining about you? Why do I have to keep getting in front of Richie and shielding you?

TOMMY: (*Getting a bit louder.*) But there you go: I'm ... they're all kind of after me.

ANGOILINO: Keep your voice down.

TOMMY: (*Lowering his voice.*) I know I'm new ... and it's like I'm being hazed. Who keeps eating the food I have in the fridge? Who keeps going through my locker? Who—

ANGOILINO: (*Interrupting.*) Nobody's going through your locker.

TOMMY: Yes, someone is.

ANGOILINO: And doing what?

TOMMY: Things have been moved around, taking things out.

ANGOILINO: Nobody's doing that, and if I ever caught anyone doing that, they'd have me to deal with. As for your food, what do you expect? It's a community fridge. Dave always eats my food. My yogurt, my salads. He uses my 2% milk for his coffee. Dave even admits it. Sometimes he throws me a few bucks.

(*Pause.*)

TOMMY: Jimmy just ... gets away with everything.

ANGOILINO: Jimmy's been here longer than you. Jimmy can show up late. Jimmy can jerk off all day ... and he does, and he gets pats on the back. Also, think: where do his parents work? Hmm? They work for the city, too. Both of them.

TOMMY: So his parents shield him.

ANGOILINO: Let's just say with him things get ignored.

TOMMY: Nobody rags on him.

ANGOILINO: I do.

TOMMY: (*Laughs.*) You rag on everybody, really.

ANGOILINO: I had to earn that. You know, when I first got on, it wasn't easy for me either. My captain at the time was a son-of-a-bitch. Thank Christ he's dead now. Never wrote me up, but he made my life a living hell. I would go home to my wife and say "I can't deal with him, I can't go in tomorrow." She seemed to think he was holding it against me that I was a Vet, but I think he was just a miserable bastard. Everything I did he had a problem with. He made me re-clean the bathrooms after I spent the afternoon cleaning them. He would wake me up in the middle of the night to take care of this or that - things that could easily been handled in the morning. When it came time to shoveling out hydrants, he sat in the truck and *I* shoveled the hydrants. Alone. I had to put the chains on. Alone. He would tell the other guys not to help me. I brought him breakfast and lunch during the day shifts and dinner during the night shifts. And this lasted past probation. It was a good - oh, close to two years.

TOMMY: What did you do?

ANGOILINO: I put up with it. What was I going to do? Beat the shit out of him? I know he wanted me to hit him. But then he'd win. (*Angoilino goes back to his chair and sits down.*) So, you have it that bad?

TOMMY: No. (*Pause.*) I don't know.

ANGOILINO: It's regret, right?

TOMMY: What?

ANGOILINO: You wished you re-upped.   Sit down. (*Tommy goes back to his chair.*) You wish you stayed.

TOMMY: ... No.

ANGOILINO: It's a lot of money they're throwing at you guys. A lot of money.

TOMMY: You know my unit's coming back next week?

ANGOILINO: That so?

TOMMY: Found out two days ago.

ANGOILINO: And...?

TOMMY: It was good to hear.

ANGOILINO: So...?

TOMMY: It was just so good to hear.

ANGOILINO: And when are they going back?

TOMMY: Oh, that ... that I don't know.

ANGOILINO: Okay.

TOMMY: I'm not sure.

ANGOILINO: Go find out.

TOMMY: Somebody will tell me.

ANGOILINO: (*Pause.*) So you regret not re-upping.

TOMMY: I don't know that it's regret.

ANGOILINO: Because I'll tell you what, you aren't 'here' now.

TOMMY: Hmm?

ANGOILINO: You're sitting here, but you're daydreaming. It's like my son's one friend. Had him on those head pills early. Just sitting at his desk - it was Catholic school. Sitting at his desk, shaking his legs. Drove the nuns up a wall.

TOMMY: (*Laughs.*) I was a public school kid.

ANGOILINO: How hard would it be to just get on the phone and sign back on?

TOMMY: What do you think I should do?

ANGOILINO: I can't tell you that. Only you can tell yourself that.

TOMMY: What would you do?

ANGOILINO: (*Thinking.*) I'm different.

TOMMY: How so?

ANGOILINO: I'm different from you. I'm a different person.

TOMMY: I know that, but I'm just asking for your advice.

ANGOILINO: I can't give you that.

(*Tommy stands up. He's getting a little disgusted.*)

TOMMY: So I can't ask your advice?

ANGOILINO: In this? No. I can give you work advice, but I can't give you advice about that.

TOMMY: You were there.

ANGOILINO: I wasn't "there." My situation was different from yours.

TOMMY: There are pros and cons to both sides.

ANGOILINO: What are your pros to going back?

TOMMY: I can't ... see, I can't explain it. My friends are there. It ... there's a *draw* to being there. An energy. It gives you ... I'm sounding stupid.

ANGOILINO: No, you aren't sounding stupid.

TOMMY: When I was there, all I thought about was coming home because I missed being home, but once I got back home ... I was glad to be home, but there was a part that just was like, "You *need* to go back."

ANGOILINO: Sure. You have good days and bad days everywhere.

TOMMY: Right.

ANGOILINO: Like here. There are good days and bad days here. There are good and bad days there. There are good and bad times everywhere. There's good in the bad. There's bad in the good. You know.

TOMMY: It should level out.

(*Angoilino stands up, mostly because he's tired of sitting.*)

ANGOILINO: What do your parents think?

TOMMY: They give me the whole "we'll support whatever you decide."

ANGOILINO: It's a great line. I've used it.

TOMMY: It's a cop-out.

ANGOILINO: (*Pause.*) How long would you re-up for?

TOMMY: Two years. Maybe.

ANGOILINO: Can you do two more years?

TOMMY: I can.

ANGOILINO: So is pay a factor?

TOMMY: They're practically begging all of us that walked away.

ANGOILINO: Obviously. You're saying your parents want you to leave here and go back there?

TOMMY: They won't give me a definite answer. That's not their way. I don't think ... I don't think they want me there. I think they want me here. Well, I do know they think this is nice, steady, secure work because they've said that already. And they're going through tough times themselves. Dad's retired. Mom never worked full-time. (*Pause.*) They were supportive when I was in high school. Dad was proud I was on the wrestling team. Told everyone. What always struck me as being weird was—

ANGOILINO: (*Interrupting.*) I wrestled in high school, too.

TOMMY: No kidding?

ANGOILINO: Three years. Go on.

TOMMY: (*Taken a little aback.*) I didn't know that. That's a really nice coincidence. What weight?

ANGOILINO: 145.

TOMMY: I was 125.

ANGOILINO: I also played football.

TOMMY: You did both?

ANGOILINO: I did. What were you saying about your Dad?

TOMMY: Oh. Well, it always seemed weird to me that no one seemed to care about my record. If I won, that was great, if I lost, that was great ... it was, you know how they say it's an 'honor to just be nominated?' It was an honor just to be on the squad. I didn't have big ambitions with it or anything like that. It's not like my high school was noted for sports. We got killed by Fullerton in everything. No one expected us to beat them or anybody else.

ANGOILINO: Who cares if no one asked about your record? Must have taken the pressure off.

TOMMY: It was like a club team. A few guys took it way too seriously ... I don't know if they thought they could get scholarships out of it or what.

ANGOILINO: So what was your record?

TOMMY: (*Thinking.*) It was okay.

ANGOILINO: .500?

TOMMY: About that. What was yours?

ANGOILINO: I don't remember those things. That was a lot of years ago.

TOMMY: Come on, you never forget that.

ANGOILINO: I did. I was better at football.

TOMMY: Tight end?

ANGOILINO: Free safety.

TOMMY: Hands were bad?

ANGOILINO: That's where they put me. (*Pause.*) So you never had plans for college?

(*Tommy lights another cigarette.*)

TOMMY: Never crossed my mind. I originally planned to just get a job someplace. Did I tell you I volunteered to pay part of my sister's college tuition?

ANGOILINO: You told me she was going but you didn't tell me that. What year is she?

TOMMY: Sophomore.

ANGOILINO: Why are you paying? Couldn't she have just gotten loans like every other kid out there?

TOMMY: I didn't want her to take out loans. She told me time and again she's pay me back but I don't expect it. Really. If she gets it and can pay me back, fine. But the money was just sitting there.

ANGOILINO: So it *is* about the money, right? To help her.

TOMMY: No, I earn enough here to help. This pays decently.

ANGOILINO: So it isn't about the money.

TOMMY: *They* pay more, don't get me wrong.

ANGOILINO: She doing okay?

TOMMY: She is.

ANGOILINO: What's she studying?

TOMMY: (*Laughs.*) English. She wants to teach.

ANGOILINO: Why would anyone *want* to do that?

TOMMY: Our aunt's a teacher. She likes it.

ANGOILINO: Gotcha. (*Tommy sits back down.*) Listen, let me just say this. (*Pause.*) I never wanted to leave. Okay, now this is me. Just me. It was a different situation, everything. My ... my family wanted me out. They hounded me. *Forced* me to leave. And that was my life. I went in at 18 ... I couldn't even drive a car. A friend of mine taught me to drive when we were stationed in Florida. Daytona. We drove on the beach. (*Pause.*) I didn't want to leave. It wasn't my decision. Everything, and you know this, everything was there for me. It's a Mom. They feed you, they dress you, they give you a job, they make sure you're healthy. They tell you when to get up. They tell you when to sleep. They tell you when to shave. You get downtime. To drink with your buddies, to play cards. You know I'm right. I *wanted* that ... I wanted that to be my career. I came back from Vietnam and it was back to ... I didn't want to come back. To (*Waves his arm in a broad gesture.*) ... to this. I was guilted into coming home and staying. Some of my relatives didn't approve of the war. Nobody ... (*Sighs.*) ... you have no idea. Nobody *here* 'got it.'

TOMMY: What do you mean "made you?"

ANGOILINO: When I came home ... I didn't talk about it with them, because they didn't want to hear it. I went to prep school, skipped class. I went to work on a garbage truck. I dug ditches. Those jobs weren't for me. Somebody told me to take the police test. I did. Passed. Also passed the fire department test. So I thought, okay. I swear to god, and now I'm too old, but if they called me I'd go. I know the recruiter on ... you know Marsh?

TOMMY: No.

ANGOILINO: Well, he's the recruiter on Tilden Street, right across from the chicken wing shop and the—

TOMMY: (*Interrupting.*) I know where you're at.

ANGOILINO: We work out at the Y. I see him there all the time. He saves the *Marine Corps Gazettes* for me. Great guy. Said he can't get kids to join, so I tell him "Send me!" and he laughs. "Anytime you want!"

TOMMY: Couldn't you go?

ANGOILINO: Don't be dumb.

TOMMY: I don't want to wake up in ten years and—

ANGOILINO: (*Interrupting.*) But that's everybody in so many things. "I shouldn't have married that woman." "I shouldn't have bought that house." "I shouldn't have had four kids." "I shouldn't have studied English in college."

TOMMY: (*Laughs.*) Right.

ANGOILINO: All things. Everybody. Think about it. I'm telling you things you know. (*Tommy stands back up, moves about lazily.*) We had a guy here at work, now this was years ago - you met Seth, right? He stops by time and again.

TOMMY: I think so. Didn't he retire early?

ANGOILINO: That's right, he did. One day he says to Richie and me, he says, "I want to fly helicopters." No military. We both laugh, sure go ahead. And goddamn it if he didn't take early retirement, go to flight school. He spends half his time down south flying around the Gulf for oil companies and the rest of the time he's back up here. Where he jogs.

TOMMY: I've seen him jogging!

ANGOILINO: I asked him, "Do you regret leaving?" And he said, and I'm quoting him, "Hell no." So you thinking you want to fly helicopters around?

TOMMY: How many years did he have in?

ANGOILINO: About ten. So what's your helicopter fantasy? Care to join the police department? You *don't* want to work in insurance—

TOMMY: (*Interrupting.*) No more college.

ANGOILINO: So what are you trained to do?

TOMMY: Keep my head down. (*Pause.*) And to get cats out of trees.

ANGOILINO: And convince people to use smoke detectors.

TOMMY: I guess I could go back and apply for a different job, get re-trained.

ANGOILINO: To what? Shouldn't you have thought of that before?

TOMMY: I liked what I did. I shouldn't have.

ANGOILINO: "Shouldn't have?" What the hell is that? I was like you. Same business. It was a job, nothing more.

(*Tommy pauses and moves away slightly from Angoilino.*)

TOMMY: You know what I wanted to be when I was a kid? You're gonna laugh. It sounds stupid. A cowboy. (*Laughs.*) Isn't that what kids in the '50s wanted to be, with *The Lone Ranger* and *Gunsmoke* and *Bonanza* and John Wayne?

ANGOILINO: Some of 'em.

TOMMY: My Dad liked John Wayne. We watched *The Green Beret* and *True Grit* and *Sands of Iwo Jima*. He also liked *Star Wars*.

ANGOILINO: I liked *Hondo*.

TOMMY: That one was good. And *The Searchers*. I mean, that's such a great image. The whole get-up and the horse and the ranch and the pistols and the wife waiting back home and the frontier and the trees.

ANGOILINO: John Wayne was a fraud.

TOMMY: He was an actor. He was charismatic. And so until I was 13 or 14 I wanted to be a cowboy.

ANGOILINO: They booed him at a USO tour.

TOMMY: I think I read about that somewhere.

ANGOILINO: Because he was a piece of shit. You know what I wanted to be as a kid?

TOMMY: The same thing?

ANGOILINO: No. I wanted to be a Marine. (*Tommy laughs.*) I had a Marine Corps Coloring Book.

TOMMY: That's pretty cool.

ANGOILINO: I had to have been 4 or 5. But I had my little Marine Corps Coloring Book, and I loved that thing. I got it from the dime store. I colored in every damn page.

TOMMY: No fireman coloring books?

ANGOILINO: I colored over those pages so much I *wore out* the pages.

TOMMY: I've always envied that. People who ... got it early. Like, they just *knew*. They didn't even think twice about anything else.

ANGOILINO: So, full circle, what are you going to do?

TOMMY: About?

ANGOILINO: Where are your car keys?

TOMMY: Excuse me?

ANGOILINO: Your car keys. Where are they?

TOMMY: I'm not sure what you mean.

ANGOILINO: Get your car keys. Drive to City Hall. Resign. Go.

TOMMY: I can't just do that.

ANGOILINO: Who says you can't?

TOMMY: You can't just do that.

ANGOILINO: (*Sarcastically.*) You can't drive your car?

TOMMY: I just can't impulsively get up and resign right now.

ANGOILINO: I just told you someone who did it.

TOMMY: I have a friend, Renzo. He lives in Delaware. He was out with me on a ... it was a Sunday night. We ... he got nailed in his chest. We got him back, took him in ... they worked on him, but the whole thing was worse than they thought. We didn't know. So before we know it, they're sending him home. He's working as a custodian at an insurance company. I saw him in the summer. His breathing is labored, he still gets severe chest pains. Has to go back for more surgeries to repair something else that was ruptured, I'm not sure exactly what. And he told me (*Laughs*) he told me that he thought it was the best revenge he could ever take, making the government pay him the rest of his life to be back here.

(*Angoilino looks at him sternly, almost taken aback. He is staring directly at Tommy. Neither speak for a while.*)

ANGOILINO: (*Growing increasingly hostile.*) What are you trying to tell me?

TOMMY: I'm just telling you about someone I know.

ANGOILINO: You're telling me this guy is glad he's injured.

TOMMY: He ... no! No, come on, I'm not saying he's *glad* he's injured, I'm saying he—

ANGOILINO: (*Interrupting.*) You're saying he's *okay with* being the way he is because then he doesn't have to go back. And he's getting paid for it, so that's good.

TOMMY: No, I'm—

ANGOILINO: (*Interrupting.*) You're telling *me* this guy wouldn't give every dollar they send him to be back to normal?

TOMMY: Maybe. Probably.

(*Angoilino steps up and stares directly at Tommy. Tommy is clearly nervous and leaning away.*)

ANGOILINO: You get. Your car keys. And you go to City Hall. And you tell them you're done. And you call Richie. And you tell *him* you're done and you tell *him* you're sorry for wasting his time. And then you stop being a burden on me and on the rest of the men.

TOMMY: (*Defensive.*) I'm sorry if I said something wrong.

ANGOILINO: You can talk around it all you want. I'm not. You have your car keys. I can see your car in the lot. You can say you like this job all you want. You say you 'like' (*waves his arm in a broad gesture*) *this*, but you don't believe it. You don't have to hear me tell you to cut the grass. You don't have to give your all here. You don't have to clean the truck. You don't have to give a little extra. You don't have to be civil with the public. You can't be late and make the person you're relieving stay for you anymore. You can't leave early to do God knows what. Sleep? Drink? I don't care.

TOMMY: You said before you weren't going to make a decision for me.

ANGOILINO: You made it for yourself. You heard yourself. So go. Go. Because you've moved yourself into this situation. It's either stay here or go back there. That's what I'm hearing. Is that what you're hearing? There are no other options. You like it 'here,' but is liking it enough? I like a lot of things. I like kayaking. I like rock climbing. They aren't careers.

TOMMY: I need time to think it over.

ANGOILINO: You've thought about it! What's left to think about?

TOMMY: I was serious ... about the positives. With staying.

ANGOILINO: Were you?

TOMMY: I was. I wouldn't just say that. It's just not as easy as just driving off.

ANGOILINO: You're hedging.

TOMMY: I'm not.

ANGOILINO: You're dancing around the subject.

TOMMY: I'll figure it out by Friday.

ANGOILINO: Oh, in three days?

TOMMY: I will.

ANGOILINO: Well, look at you! Three days!

TOMMY: You're making fun of me.

ANGOILINO: No. (*Pause. Angoilino is looking hard at Tommy. He then starts to walk back to the station.*) I'm getting some more coffee. Gonna find out about the house fire and what company seven's doing. Get in here and get the keys to the mower. (*Angoilino exits. Tommy is standing still. He doesn't respond. In a few moments Angoilino steps back on stage.*) Bring my chair in.

(*Angoilino exits again.*)

(*Tommy takes a little bit of time. He goes over to both chairs and closes them up. As he begins to take them off-stage, he notices the small half-full bag of acorns still sitting on the ground. He sets down the chairs, picks up the bag, opens it up and dumps the rest of the acorns all over the stage, scattering a select few with his boot. He then tucks the empty bag into his pocket, grabs both lawn chairs and exits.*)

CURTAIN.

The Cut-Paper Shadow

A Play in One Act

2015

CHARACTERS

Gwendolyn, a resident of OpenHands Nursing Home. She is in her early 80's.

Constance, Gwendolyn's daughter. She is in her mid-50's.

Adrianna, a nurse

Glenn, a resident of OpenHands Nursing Home. He is in his late 70's.

Place: A meeting area inside the OpenHands Nursing Home

Time: A summer afternoon, early August.

(*Inside the OpenHands Nursing Home is a meeting area that has a single circular table in the center of the room surrounded by four chairs. In the back of the room is a kiosk for coffee (there are two pots, Styrofoam cups, a bowl for sweeteners, stirrers and a small carton of milk) and one vending machine with soft drinks in it. There is one door situated stage left. Sunshine beams in through the windows located stage right.*

A nurse at OpenHands, Adrianna, comes into the room.)

ADRIANNA: Okay, Gwen, easy now. (*Gwendolyn enters right behind the nurse. She moves slowly, so Adrianna holds her left arm gently to make sure she doesn't fall and then helps her get into her chair at the end of the table.*) You have a visitor today. Excited?

GWENDOLYN: It depends on who it is.

ADRIANNA: (*Smiling.*) It's your daughter!

GWENDOLYN: ... Oh! Good! I was going to— (*Just as Gwendolyn is speaking Constance, her daughter, enters the room.*) —ah, there you are!

CONSTANCE: Hi, Mom. Hi, Adrianna.

ADRIANNA: Your Mom had an exciting day yesterday, we had a bowling tournament and she came in second place.

GWENDOLYN: Always second place! That good for nothing Betty or Betsy, she's almost a pro. She wins it every time.

ADRIANNA: You'll get her next time! Anyway, I have to go, just a reminder you have physical therapy at 3:30.

GWENDOLYN: I do? My back is better.

ADRIANNA: That's good, but we have to make sure it's *really* strong, don't want you to fall again. (*Slight pause.*) Bye, Connie. (*She makes a waving motion to Connie and exits.*)

GWENDOLYN: She's a nice girl. A flirt with the men but a nice girl.

CONSTANCE: I think the staff here does their best.

GWENDOLYN: (*Pause.*) You haven't been here in a while.

CONSTANCE: I was here a little over two weeks ago. It's been a busy time with Jeannie going off to college soon.

GWENDOLYN: She's going to love it, she's got it together.

CONSTANCE: We sent you an invite for her graduation party and volunteered to come get you for it but they said your back was too bad.

GWENDOLYN: (*Thinking.*) Yes, it was. Bad. How long ago was that?

CONSTANCE: Two months ago.

GWENDOLYN: Because Jeannie hasn't been to see me in a while.

CONSTANCE: She has.

GWENDOLYN: When?

CONSTANCE: After the party we brought her over here.

GWENDOLYN: Oh, right, right. Those pills they give you, they drug you up so you don't move or think. I feel like I sleep all day!

CONSTANCE: But you're off them now?

GWENDOLYN: I take a bunch in the morning. I don't even ask what they all are anymore. Had blood work done, they said this is too high, this is too low, who even knows what they're on about.

CONSTANCE: What's too high?

GWENDOLYN: I don't know, I don't even listen. They speak in mumbo-jumbo. I don't think they know how to fix anybody.

CONSTANCE: Because you had syncope. [*pronounced 'SING-kə-pee'*]

GWENDOLYN: What's that?

CONSTANCE: That's what they called your fainting spells.

GWENDOLYN: I'm fine! I just get light-headed sometimes. Don't you ever get light-headed?

CONSTANCE: (*Hesitant.*) Sometimes.

GWENDOLYN: See, it's hereditary.

CONSTANCE: (*Half-grimacing.*) That's not very re-assuring.

GWENDOLYN: You get old, things happen. (*She shrugs.*)

(*There's a long pause.*)

CONSTANCE: The real reason I'm here is to tell you that, and I didn't want to say it over the phone, but Dad died last night.

GWENDOLYN: (*Shocked.*) Peter died? Oh my God, no!

CONSTANCE: No, Mom. *My* Dad. (*Pause.*) Louis. (*Pause.*) Your first husband.

GWENDOLYN: (*Annoyed.*) I know who he is! I'm not an idiot!

CONSTANCE: I just thought you should know, and I wanted to tell you in person.

GWENDOLYN: Of course I needed to know! We spent 15 years together. He helped give me you. (*Thinking.*) Was he sick?

CONSTANCE: He had a stroke.

GWENDOLYN: (*Pause.*) He always did drink too much.

CONSTANCE: (*Annoyed.*) Dad quit drinking over twenty years ago. He even attended AA.

GWENDOLYN: Well. I'm sorry to hear that. (*Pause.*) I haven't seen him in so long. (*Thinking.*) Last I saw him in person we ran into each other at the Fair, had to have been, oh, I don't remember when. I was listening to the jazz band and talking with friends and he walked near me. I called out for him and he looked at me and scowled and walked away. So much time had passed, I wanted to know how he was doing. He could have said something.

CONSTANCE: Why do you think he should have said anything?

GWENDOLYN: (*Slapping her palms on the table lightly.*) Fifteen years! We spent fifteen years together!

CONSTANCE: How many of those years were you actually together.

GWENDOLYN: Don't start with that, he walked out on me.

CONSTANCE: (*Stunned.*) You can't be serious.

GWENDOLYN: He was going to lunches and dinners with that ... what's her face. The *typist*. (*Constance registers disgust at this response.*) Everyone acting like I didn't know.

CONSTANCE: I ... I can't believe you're doing this right now.

GWENDOLYN: Doing what?

CONSTANCE: Flipping the story around like I'm the one who doesn't understand. (*She takes a long pause to collect herself.*) Do you want coffee? I'm going to get some coffee.

(*Constance gets up to go over to the coffee kiosk and starts pouring a cup for herself.*) Do you want any?

GWENDOLYN: No, I don't. (*Constance returns to her seat.*) Flipping what around? He divorced me.

CONSTANCE: I guess this means you have no interest in going to the viewing or funeral to say your goodbyes.

GWENDOLYN: We were fighting a lot. He stayed out late many nights.

CONSTANCE: (*Sighs.*) You were starting the fights. He worked with a lot of people and they were all out late. He took overtime to support us because you weren't working steadily.

GWENDOLYN: You're so gullible, he could always snow you.

CONSTANCE: You needed an excuse to run off with Peter and turned and made it look like it was Dad's fault.

GWENDOLYN: (*Shaking her head.*) I don't know where you're coming up with this.

CONSTANCE: Dad was too "boring" for you. You needed your "freedom." I listened from my room. I heard what you were saying.

GWENDOLYN: (*Insistent.*) I never said that. You were a child, you wouldn't have understood.

CONSTANCE: I was a freshman in high school. Yes, I was young, but I know what I heard.

GWENDOLYN: And I wouldn't have called him "boring."

CONSTANCE: Can we just drop it?

GWENDOLYN: I don't know what ever made you hate me. You never liked me.

CONSTANCE: Hate you? I'm here visiting you, right?

GWENDOLYN: You held it against me that I was the tough one. He let you do anything you want. Run around. He got you out of that problem at that party.

CONSTANCE: He was a Dad to me. He was always there for me. When you ran off—

GWENDOLYN: (*Interrupting.*) I did not run off.

CONSTANCE: When you ... left both of us he was there for me. Were you at *my* high school graduation?

GWENDOLYN: (*Thinking.*) I was on tour. Theater work involves a lot of travel. You knew what I did for a living.

CONSTANCE: Were you at *my* college graduation?

GWENDOLYN: (*Thinking.*) I sent a card and a cheque.

CONSTANCE: If you did I never saw it.

GWENDOLYN: Your father probably ripped it up.

CONSTANCE: Or my wedding? When did you ever call?

GWENDOLYN: I did try a few times but your father or husband or whoever kept hanging up on me.

CONSTANCE: When I tried getting a hold of you I always got Peter or some other person and they were always "taking messages" for you, whatever that means. You were "supposedly" never in the room when I tried to reach you.

GWENDOLYN: I take it you've never been busy before in your whole life?

CONSTANCE: You never made an effort. It took you being put in here a year ago for me to know where you are most of the time. And *then* I only knew about it because *I* made an effort to find you and *I* made the effort to drive over here and see you. Your old landlord told me what happened, about how Peter had to be put in a nursing home five years ago and about all the wandering you were doing, the rundown condition of the apartment—

GWENDOLYN: (*Interrupting.*) What wandering? I was looking for my car.

CONSTANCE: You were in your delicates, Mom.

GWENDOLYN: (*Dismissive.*) That's just the police being dirty old men, I was trying to find my car, I didn't remember where I parked it.

CONSTANCE: They couldn't believe you were still driving.

GWENDOLYN: I was driving just fine. I have the start of cataracts in both my eyes, it just makes it tough to see at night but otherwise, no tickets or accidents.

CONSTANCE: The car had a few dents in it.

GWENDOLYN: It was basically brand new!

CONSTANCE: It was six years old and had dents and scratches all over it. Garbage was piling up in the backseat.

GWENDOLYN: I know that car was fine.

CONSTANCE: It was not fine because we had to sell it for you.

GWENDOLYN: (*Shocked.*) You sold my car on me? When? Why didn't you tell me?

(*At that moment another resident of the nursing home, Glenn, enters. He has a walker but doesn't seem to need it - it's more of a hindrance to him than anything. Gwendolyn sees him and is annoyed.*)

GLENN: Well! My favorite lady and her daughter! How are both of you this afternoon?

CONSTANCE: (*Suddenly less annoyed and struggling to smile.*) Hey Glenn, how are things?

GLENN: So-so. Taking it a day at a time.

CONSTANCE: Heart's still giving you problems?

GLENN: Ehh, it's beating. Badly, but it's beating. Had a run to the hospital last week.

GWENDOLYN: Glenn, we're trying to—

GLENN: (*Oblivious to Gwendolyn's speaking.*) I was lying in bed and all of a sudden it felt like someone was standing on my chest. It began tightening up again. So I tell the Nurse, the tall one with red hair, and they send me out. Two days in the hospital and discharged. They don't want to keep you, do they? "Go die somewhere else." It wasn't a heart attack, which is good, but now I have even more medications and a more restricted diet. (*He leans in and almost whispers.*) I love ice cream. And chips. And cake. I shouldn't but ... (*He laughs.*) Old habits die hard!

GWENDOLYN: (*Annoyed.*) Don't you have somewhere to be?

GLENN: Just came in for my soda! (*To Constance, again almost whispering.*) Another vice!

(*Glenn reaches in his pocket for change and then struggles to get over to the soda vending machine. He drops the change all over the floor.*)

CONSTANCE: I'll help, hold on. (*She gets up and picks up the change and puts it in the machine for Glenn.*) Which one do you want? (*Glenn pushes the button on the console and the can comes out. She picks the soda up for him and hands it to him.*)

GLENN: Thank you! (*Smiling.*) These damn hands! (*Pause.*) Say, Gwen, did you tell your daughter about the concert you had for us on Sunday?

CONSTANCE: What concert?

GWENDOLYN: It was no big deal.

GLENN: She did a whole medley for us in the Great Room! All those old classics. "I Got Rhythm," oh, and that other Judy Garland—

GWENDOLYN: (*Interrupting.*) It was a nice night and I'm glad I can still do something with my voice. Don't you need to go somewhere?

GLENN: (*To Constance.*) Can you believe how many famous people she's met! That story about Tony Curtis was simply fantastic!

CONSTANCE: (*To Gwendolyn.*) When did you meet Tony Curtis?

GWENDOLYN: I've met a lot of people.

GLENN: Your mother is an absolute gem. The other residents love her, she can make anyone's day. Such a lady! I feel like I get to live with a celebrity.

CONSTANCE: (*Sarcastically.*) She does have quite the story.

GWENDOLYN: (*Proudly.*) I met Sinatra at a party once. He was so magnetic, everyone in the room was electrified by him. Could hold his booze. Wow. We had dinner with Bob Fosse and his floozies a couple of times. I even got to work with Jerome Robbins, who was a very charming man. My husband was good friends with him.

GLENN: (*To Constance.*) Your father must have been well connected!

(*Pause.*)

CONSTANCE: She's talking about her second husband. My Dad was her first husband.

GLENN: (*Suddenly uncomfortable.*) I'm sorry. I didn't know.

GWENDOLYN: He just passed and we're making arrangements for his funeral.

(*Constance gives Gwendolyn a cutting glance.*)

GLENN: (*Embarrassed.*) Oh, I'm interrupting you two. Sorry for your loss. I'll be going.

CONSTANCE: It's no trouble at all. No need to rush.

GLENN: Take care ladies, all the best.

CONSTANCE: Thanks, Glenn.

(*Glenn exits.*)

GWENDOLYN: I have lots of fans here. People who appreciate me.

CONSTANCE: You were a little short with Glenn.

GWENDOLYN: He saw we were talking and kept going on and wouldn't take the hint. I don't interrupt him when he meets with his partner. At dinner he sometimes sits at our table and won't stop talking. None of us can get a word in edge-wise!

CONSTANCE: Maybe it's his way of being friendly.

GWENDOLYN: (*Rolling her eyes.*) *Hmph.*

CONSTANCE: Well, Mom ... (*She gets up.*) I need to go. I have to make some phone calls and take care of a few things. Now if you change your mind about—

GWENDOLYN: (*Interrupting.*) Where do you think you're going? You never told me what you did with my car.

CONSTANCE: (*To herself.*) *This again.* (*She sits back down.*) I told you that the car had to be sold. We had to sell most of your things.

GWENDOLYN: What about my photo albums and scrapbooks? My collection of watercolor paintings?

CONSTANCE: A lot of that is in storage.

GWENDOLYN: Where is my jewelry? I had several tennis bracelets and all those diamond earrings. I don't think those are in my room.

CONSTANCE: If you had it and it was salvageable, it's in storage. The car had to be sold.

GWENDOLYN: Well, I want my things back! How can I get to them if they're in storage?

CONSTANCE: (*Frustrated.*) I don't have time to get those things right now and I don't think you have room to put them. (*Collecting herself.*) Right now I have to deal with Dad's belongings and Will and ... I just have to take care of things for him right now, okay?

GWENDOLYN: Why doesn't one of his *typists* do that? You shouldn't have to do that.

CONSTANCE: (*Annoyed.*) *Typists*? Really? He was living alone. He was allergic to dogs so he couldn't have one with him for company. Never liked cats. Jeannie or I would visit and bring him dinner. He watched a lot of pro wrestling. He read old Westerns. Fished a lot.

GWENDOLYN: Did you or Jeannie ever bring me dinner?

CONSTANCE: They have a cafeteria here. Dad didn't have a cafeteria. He lived by himself.

GWENDOLYN: I always figured some floozy was living with him.

CONSTANCE: (*Stunned.*) You want to know something? I'll tell you something. He went on a total of two dates after your divorce that I know about. Neither were *typists*. When I went and got married and moved out, he lived alone. (*Pause.*) You were the last for him.

(*Gwendolyn doesn't say anything. Constance gets up to leave again.*)

GWENDOLYN: Why didn't he call me or talk to me, then? Why did he fight with me so much? He could have tried connecting with me.

CONSTANCE: (*She sits back down. She closes her eyes.*) Mom.

GWENDOLYN: You remember how we met right?

CONSTANCE: (*Sighing.*) Yes, I know the story.

GWENDOLYN: We met after he saw me in *Blithe Spirit*. I played Ruth. He was there with some other broad. But he found me in the lobby after the show and he said to me, "You were a dream on stage." He said that. The way he looked at me ... it was something. (*Thinking.*) Then, it was two nights later, he was there again ... and this time he was alone. He asked me if I was seeing anybody. I said no. Of course I was. But the way he looked - he was in uniform, how he loved to traipse around in that - I thought it was worth a shot. He got me a drink, we talked, we walked. One thing after another, he said he'd follow me to the ends of the Earth. *The ends of the Earth.* He told me that. Swore on it. As time went by ... he became less interested in me.

CONSTANCE: (*In disbelief.*) So you're saying that you believe the two feel you grew apart. Okay.

GWENDOLYN: He had a wandering eye.

CONSTANCE: You keep saying this like you're trying to convince me you're right and he's wrong. I only knew you for a short period of time. I've spent almost every day of my life leading up to today in communication with him. He was a good man. He was there for my daughter's birth. He was there for my brother-in-law's funeral. He was there for my best friend's wedding. (*Laughs, thinking.*) My friends invited him to picnics and sometimes forgot to invite me. He had his faults. The drinking got bad and he got into a few bar brawls. Normally mothers covet their children, and you acted like I never existed once you got your hands on Peter or whoever could help your career.

GWENDOLYN: Not only is that nonsense, it's disgusting. It's crazy. You were ... you were brainwashed.

CONSTANCE: Fine, it's crazy. I'm going to go. (*She tries to get up once again.*)

GWENDOLYN: Stay. Wait. (*Pause.*) You're my only child.

CONSTANCE: (*Standing.*) Okay, so I am. Right now, that means what?

GWENDOLYN: You're one of the last I have left.

CONSTANCE: Right, you have Peter.

GWENDOLYN: (*Looking down.*) They can't even bring him to see me.

CONSTANCE: Why is that?

GWENDOLYN: Last I was told he was too bad off. I keep trying to get the staff here to call up the place he's at but they don't get a response. He didn't remember me when I visited him last.

CONSTANCE: That's bad.

GWENDOLYN: He took me for his sister. I had to tell him I wasn't. I told him his sister was gone. He started crying.

CONSTANCE: It sounds like it's really advanced.

GWENDOLYN: (*Solemnly.*) Yes. We had good times.

CONSTANCE: (*Pandering.*) I'm glad you did.

GWENDOLYN: But you don't want to hear about that. I know. I'm talking so much about myself. I didn't even think to ask about you. What else is new with you. Aside from the bad news. Anything good?

CONSTANCE: (*Finally sitting back down.*) Work is fine, school starts up in a couple of weeks so I have to prepare the classroom and get a few books and assignments together.

GWENDOLYN: Do you like teaching?

CONSTANCE: I do, even after all these years of doing it. The kids are fun, they keep you sharp. Many of the other teachers are supportive. You get into a routine.

GWENDOLYN: High school?

CONSTANCE: Middle school. Tough transitional time for them, so you have to stay firm. We get into radio plays and Shakespeare, the kids do a musical at the end of the year.

GWENDOLYN: Ha! So we do have something in common.

CONSTANCE: (*A little taken aback.*) I guess, a little. The boys can be a handful and goofy, the girls are usually a step up on them in maturity.

GWENDOLYN: Not planning on retiring?

CONSTANCE: Oh no, not yet. I'll know when it's time to be done with it.

GWENDOLYN: And the rest of your family?

CONSTANCE: I told you about Jeannie. She's nervous about the move to school but she's excited. The husband is good, he tore his meniscus boxing—

GWENDOLYN: (*Interrupting.*) I never met him did I?

CONSTANCE: No, no you haven't.

GWENDOLYN: What does he look like? (*Thinking.*) I don't know if you showed me.

(*Constance reaches in her purse and takes out her phone. She finds a photo on her phone and hands it to her.*)

CONSTANCE: This is a newer one. (*Pause.*) He's on the left.

GWENDOLYN: He's burly!

CONSTANCE: (*Smiling.*) He has gained some weight but he's on a doctor-ordered diet.

(*Gwendolyn hands her the phone back.*)

GWENDOLYN: Only husband?

CONSTANCE: We've been married 19 years now.

GWENDOLYN: Big Twenty coming up!

CONSTANCE: We figure we'll go to Miami next summer to celebrate, he really likes those jet-skis. Jeannie likes the beach. We haven't gone on many vacations.

GWENDOLYN: I really would like to meet him. You should bring him over here, I'd like to talk to him. You sound like you picked a good one.

CONSTANCE: (*Suddenly reserved.*) We'll see.

GWENDOLYN: (*Pause, concerned.*) Why the hesitation?

CONSTANCE: What hesitation?

GWENDOLYN: You don't want to bring him to see me?

CONSTANCE: He works long hours and has to help with his own aging parents and—

GWENDOLYN: (*Interrupting*) So he can't come with you even for an hour to meet me? It would be nice to at least see the man married to my daughter. I met Jeannie.

CONSTANCE: I'll talk to him.

GWENDOLYN: Talk to him about ... what?

CONSTANCE: I'll see if I can convince him to come.

GWENDOLYN: Convince him? What's to convince?

CONSTANCE: Mom.

GWENDOLYN: He doesn't want to meet me. That's it.

CONSTANCE: He has a lot of ... friends and hobbies and—

GWENDOLYN: (*Interrupting.*) You poisoned him against me.

CONSTANCE: (*Stunned.*) I did not. Jeannie's been here.

GWENDOLYN: I'm not talking about her. I'm talking about your husband.

CONSTANCE: (*Long pause.*) He was close with Dad...

GWENDOLYN: (*Angry.*) He did it to me again!

CONSTANCE: Did what?

GWENDOLYN: Your father. Poisoning people against me.

CONSTANCE: (*Restrained.*) He liked Dad a lot. They went fishing. They were close. I don't know what they talked about and I'm sure you weren't the only thing they discussed.

GWENDOLYN: Your father told everyone I'm some kind of loon and then made them all like him and told lies and kept us apart so many years.

CONSTANCE: He probably told him what he felt and—

GWENDOLYN: (*Interrupting.*) And what did you tell him?

CONSTANCE: (*Sighing.*) Mom.

GWENDOLYN: You told him the same thing. Did you even for a second consider it from my viewpoint?

CONSTANCE: That's not how it works. Over time you sort of ... make your own viewpoint and—

GWENDOLYN: (*Interrupting.*) Then I'm going to set the record straight. Bring your husband here. I just want to talk to him and set him straight.

CONSTANCE: (*Sternly.*) He doesn't like you.

GWENDOLYN: He doesn't know me! He needs to hear about the *typists* and the late nights—

CONSTANCE: (*Interrupting.*) I'll work on that. Okay? I'll work on that.

GWENDOLYN: And bring Jeannie too, I want both of them here so I can settle this once and for all.

CONSTANCE: (*Getting up.*) I have to go to the bathroom.

GWENDOLYN: You're trying to wiggle out of this. You can't just hear one side and think you have it all right.

CONSTANCE: (*Walking to the door.*) I will see what I can do.

GWENDOLYN: Don't go yet, we're not done here. This doesn't feel settled.

CONSTANCE: I really need to use the bathroom.

GWENDOLYN: Go and then come back. I'll be in here. (*Constance leaves. Pause. Gwendolyn mutters to herself softly.*) That bastard.

(*Gwendolyn sits waiting for a period of time. She eyes the coffee kiosk, gets up gingerly and pours herself a cup and adds milk. She carefully returns to her seat. Constance has*

*not returned but her coffee cup remains on the table.
Gwendolyn takes a taste of her own cup of coffee and
grimaces and slides the coffee away from her on the table.
More time passes. She remains seated and waiting.*

Adrianna enters.)

ADRIANNA: Gwen! It's time for your physical therapy.

GWENDOLYN: (*Surprised.*) What time is it?

ADRIANNA: It's close to 3:00. But we have to walk all the
way over there and we don't want to be late!

GWENDOLYN: I told you I'm feeling better.

ADRIANNA: (*Smiling.*) We know, but you're about 95%
and we want you to get to 100%!

GWENDOLYN: So only a few more times?

ADRIANNA: I'll let the physical therapist set a timeline. It
should only be a couple more we think.

GWENDOLYN: Couple more? How many is that?
(*Adrianna helps Gwendolyn out of her chair.*)

ADRIANNA: Just a few, it's not too painful is it?

GWENDOLYN: No, not at all!

ADRIANNA: When it gets perfectly healed you can get first
place in bowling!

(*The two start to make their way to the exit. Gwendolyn stops.*)

GWENDOLYN: (*Pause.*) Remember I did my little concert for everybody?

ADRIANNA: Of course I do, it was a big hit with everybody!

GWENDOLYN: Did you like it?

ADRIANNA: I was only able to catch part of it but you sounded amazing. How many years did it take you to get that good?

GWENDOLYN: So many! It takes a lot of practice. Longer than you've been around!

ADRIANNA: No doubt.

GWENDOLYN: Do you think we should do it again? Schedule another one?

ADRIANNA: (*Smiling.*) Absolutely! But right now it's time for your physical therapy. You need a healthy body to sing!

GWENDOLYN: Will you be able to make it for the show?

ADRIANNA: Depends on when it is, but I'll try not to miss it!

GWENDOLYN: Good. I'll see if I can change it up a bit and get some new numbers in there to keep it from being stale.

ADRIANNA: We'll all be looking forward to it!

(*They exit.*)

CURTAIN.

Silver Light, Good Morning

A Play in One Act

2019

CHARACTERS

Oliver

Zinnia

Place: Oliver's studio apartment.

Time: Early July.

* Note: The light from the bay window transitions from bright gray at the beginning to bright yellow-orange at the end.

(*In Oliver's apartment there is a king size bed in the middle of the main living space and it is close to a large bay window, left, which looks out onto the street below. Next to the bed are a few bottles of wine and empty beer cans. On the walls are framed photographs and a couple of prints of fine art. There is a night stand on Oliver's side with a digital clock turned away from the audience. Stage right is the kitchen area - with a microwave, a coffee machine, a refrigerator, a stove and several medicine bottles - as well as the bathroom and the door to exit to the hallway. Articles of clothing are strewn about the floor.*

Zinnia wakes up. She looks next to her, sees Oliver is still asleep and crawls out of bed carefully. She is not wearing any clothing, so she searches around for something to put on and can only locate her panties and Oliver's polo shirt. Zinnia goes over to the collection of books on the shelves beneath the bay window and takes a few items, examines them closely, and places them back where she found them.

She goes over to the record collection in the corner, takes out a record, places it on the player and starts playing it on a low volume. Oliver hears it and struggles to raise his head.)

OLIVER: Are you up already?

ZINNIA: I turned over and got dizzy. Then I started sweating a little.

OLIVER: Oh ... okay. (*He lays back on the pillow, checks the time and moves the clock back to facing the wall.*) It's early. We have to sleep it off.

(*Zinnia, examining the record sleeve, walks over to the wine bottles, shakes them to see which ones are full and takes the one that's half full back to the record player and sits down. She takes a long pull from the bottle and sets it down.*)

ZINNIA: This record ... it says it was released in 1974 but recorded in 1973. I wonder how many band guys from then had long hair. (*Oliver doesn't respond.*) I feel like there's something interesting about guys with long hair, you know? It's got this whole rebellious-but-in-touch-with-my-feminine-side thing about it.

OLIVER: (*Slightly mumbling.*) Glam rock was big around then. There was this androgynous feel to it all. It extended to the 80's hair metal bands like Whitesnake and Def Leppard. (*Pause.*) The Ramones also had long hair although they were punks. But I'm not a rock historian.

ZINNIA: It's got this whole *fuck you and everything about you* attitude. I get that. (*She takes another pull off the bottle.*)

(*Oliver shifts around in bed but he can't go back to sleep.*)

OLIVER: Turn it off and let's get a few more hours. I need it.

(*She ignores his request.*)

ZINNIA: You never had a long-hair phase did you?

OLIVER: No. Never cared to.

ZINNIA: When did you start collecting vinyl? You've got so many. And books too.

OLIVER: I don't know. My grandmother bought me a record player when I was little and every Christmas would give me a couple new albums. She used to sing in a band. She tried to teach me piano, but I wasn't interested in practicing. (*Long Pause.*) I should have followed her advice.

ZINNIA: Think it's too late for me to start? Can you see me as a bassist?

OLIVER: You might be good on bass. I don't know, pick up a used one and get a beginner's guide. A lot of great musicians were self-taught. It probably helps if you have some innate musical aptitude.

ZINNIA: None of my relatives are musically inclined. I'm probably screwed in that department.

OLIVER: You never know unless you try. (*He tries getting out of bed. He sits on the edge, staring at the floor.*) Oh, oh shit ... I'm dizzy.

ZINNIA: (*Getting up and handing him the bottle.*) Have a swig. I read an article about drinking in the morning to get rid of the hangover.

(*He takes two quick swallows and gives her the bottle back. There's a long pause.*)

OLIVER: Nope. That ... nope. (*He stumbles to the bathroom without clothes on and slams the door.*)

(*Zinnia goes over to the bathroom door and gives a light knock.*)

ZINNIA: Are you all right? I know you drank more than me. (*Oliver can be heard coughing and gagging.*) Are you going to be okay? Need me to come in?

OLIVER: No. Just wait. (*He keeps coughing, with each cough getting louder.*) Gimme a second.

ZINNIA: (*Setting the bottle of wine on the counter.*) Do you want me to drive to the drug store to get you anything?

OLIVER: (*Spitting up.*) You're in a condition to drive?

ZINNIA: Damn it. Good point.

OLIVER: Just wait. It will be all right. (*The toilet flushes. The sound of gargling can be heard as well as the sink running.*)

ZINNIA: Maybe I can walk from here? It shouldn't be too far to ... maybe a convenience store or someplace like that. Just give me a list of what you need.

(*Oliver exits the bathroom with a towel wrapped around his waist.*)

OLIVER: What happened was ... wow, am I sweating. I had to get that out of me. Hope I wasn't too loud. (*Pause.*) Now I need to take two Advil and drink some juice. (*He takes apple juice out of the refrigerator and opens the bottle of Advil and swallows two pills, washing them down with the juice out of the container.*) So what happened was, I started drinking here earlier—

ZINNIA: (*Interrupting.*) You left your apartment drunk?

OLIVER: Buzzed. I was just buzzed. It was only beer. A couple beers, if I'm going to be honest. So then I left here, and I was supposed to meet with my friend Andrew but he's working overtime. Overtime on a Friday ... what the hell. And there are plenty of restaurants in this neighborhood, so I was thinking, "I need to eat something." It's just me, right, but you know that Daniel Halpern line about how eating alone is the best company you will ever have? So I see you outside waiting tables and I'm thinking, why not stop in here? (*Pause.*) Sorry, I'm being rude. Would you like some juice? Maybe coffee? I have milk, too.

ZINNIA: No, I'm good right now. You mean you had no idea I worked there.

OLIVER: I'm ... maybe? I'm not sure.

ZINNIA: Because I did mention it to you a couple of times.

OLIVER: I guess you did, but ... maybe it just sort of lodged itself in the back of my memory? (*Pause.*) Would you mind turning off the record player? It's still going.

ZINNIA: It's not loud at all.

OLIVER: My neighbors have supersonic hearing. And it's early. And they probably hear us chatting loudly. (*Pause.*) Please.

ZINNIA: (*Sighing.*) Fine. (*She goes over and turns it off.*) Happy, mister?

OLIVER: (*Wincing slightly.*) Thank you. Much appreciated.

ZINNIA: So you forgot I worked there and walked by and saw me and you were like, "Huh, how about that. There's Zin."

OLIVER: I'm not sure I would put it like that.

ZINNIA: You weren't ... seeking me out?

OLIVER: No. Absolutely not.

ZINNIA: Because it seemed like that's just what happened.

OLIVER: Pure coincidence. (*Pause.*) Maybe an educated coincidence. But I recall you telling me the food was well above average and you had decent rapport with the owner and the rest of the staff.

ZINNIA: I did. Now you're remembering.

OLIVER: Okay. So, hold on a minute. (*Pause.*) I recall you telling me you started in October. Just before Halloween. And then you said you got in trouble for moving kegs around? Something about the police seeing you rolling them across the street?

ZINNIA: Ding ding ding.

OLIVER: You also mentioned the one bartender going through a bad divorce, someone else there got a laughably bad tattoo of what was supposed to be a unicorn but looked like a yak, there was a Christmas party that got a little weird....

ZINNIA: All right, so you were paying attention.

OLIVER: See? Told you. I'm just ... it's a little fuzzy right about now. Are you sure you don't want coffee?

ZINNIA: No, not right now. You asked the hostess if you could be seated in my section, is that true?

OLIVER: It is. I did. I thought, hey, why not? I left a nice tip.

ZINNIA: And you asked me when my shift ended, and if I'd like to talk some more.

OLIVER: (*Hesitantly.*) I did.

ZINNIA: Was it the beer talking?

OLIVER: I don't know. It might have been. I'm not the most ... open person sober.

ZINNIA: I get that. And then you asked when my shift was over, and I said after closing.

OLIVER: You gave me a free dessert. Lemon meringue.

ZINNIA: That's true. That was on me.

OLIVER: (*Pause.*) Thank you for that.

ZINNIA: Happy to be of assistance.

(*There's a long pause.*)

OLIVER: Did ... am I wrong in asking if you had a good time? I enjoyed your company.

ZINNIA: It was very ... different.

OLIVER: Because ... (*Rubs his face.*) ... I'm making coffee. (*He prepares the coffee maker with fresh grounds.*) If you want some, there'll be plenty for both of us.

ZINNIA: All right.

(*Pause.*)

OLIVER: (*Checking the counter and the refrigerator.*) Do I have any wine left? We drank everything?

ZINNIA: We went through an entire vineyard. (*Pointing to the bottle on the counter.*) This one is about half full.

OLIVER: Almost my whole supply. Impressive. (*Pause.*) I shouldn't have mixed everything together. That was amateur hour.

ZINNIA: (*Pause.*) It's interesting seeing you like this. Very different from the chirpy Mr. Whitehall I'm used to seeing first thing in the morning.

OLIVER: I can assure you, this is ... not the usual me. That is the usual me. But this summer, I don't know. I've just been doing a lot of thinking. Probably too much thinking. I'm the kind of person that needs to keep busy. Always have to keep ... doing things, you know? (*Pause.*) Are you hungry? Do you want eggs? I think I have eggs ... (*He opens up the refrigerator.*) ... I do, eggs and ... (*Checks counter.*) ... three bagels. So how about it, eggs and a bagel as my trade for your dessert.

ZINNIA: I'm not that hungry, so make mine a half a bagel.

OLIVER: That sounds good. I'll have the other half.

(*While Oliver makes breakfast, cracking the eggs and getting out the butter and toasting the bagels, Zinnia takes the wine bottle off the counter and takes sips while looking around the apartment. The bright grey night is slowly turning bright red.*)

ZINNIA: Can I ask you something?

OLIVER: (*Hesitantly.*) Depends on what it is.

ZINNIA: How can you afford this nice a place in the center of town on your salary? I hope that doesn't come off wrong.

OLIVER: No, good question. Honest question. How do you know how much I make?

ZINNIA: My uncle is a teacher. But he's in Delaware. I just thought it was common knowledge that teachers got paid like shit.

OLIVER: It's a living. (*Pause.*) Do you mind if your eggs are scrambled?

ZINNIA: That's fine. Do you have ketchup?

OLIVER: Ketchup? For what?

ZINNIA: The eggs.

OLIVER: You don't put ketchup on eggs.

ZINNIA: I do. What's wrong with it?

OLIVER: (*Checking fridge.*) I have ketchup. But ugh, that's ... not the way to eat eggs.

ZINNIA: You didn't say how you were able to afford this place.

OLIVER: Right, that. Well ... my parents they, um ... they own this whole building.

ZINNIA: Get out! So you're living here rent-free?

OLIVER: Not entirely. I pay the utilities. (*Pause.*) I'm fortunate in that regard. But it's a complicated story. I have an older brother ... he's ... more of what my parents wanted. He studied the right things, he got the breaks. I just wanted to teach, I like the energy of a classroom engaged, which isn't often. To have time to travel. They groomed me to take over their business and here I am ... not doing that.

ZINNIA: You're doing what you want. There's nothing wrong with that.

OLIVER: It's led to some tough arguments.

ZINNIA: I had to fight with my parents to even apply to art school. They wanted me to study biology or chemistry or something like that. They said to me, "Do you want to starve?" And I'm like, isn't that an extreme over-reaction?

OLIVER: I remember how happy you were when you got in to your first choice. In New York, no less. They're giving you financial aid, aren't they?

ZINNIA: Some. Not a lot.

(*The toaster pops.*)

OLIVER: Bagel's ready. I don't have cream cheese. Is butter okay?

ZINNIA: That's good.

(*Oliver spreads butter on the bagel and hands Zinnia's half to her on a paper towel. She sets the bottle of wine on the floor.*)

OLIVER: Coffee? I only have milk.

ZINNIA: Do you have sugar?

OLIVER: You put sugar in your coffee?

ZINNIA: Who are you, Tony Bourdain? Let me drink what I want how I want it.

OLIVER: (*Sighing.*) Fine. (*He puts a teaspoon of sugar in her coffee and some milk.*) Here's your sweetened blend. (*He hands her a colorful mug.*)

ZINNIA: Thank you.

OLIVER: Eggs coming up next.

ZINNIA: I see you have all these nice photographs on your walls. Did you take them?

OLIVER: Some, yes. Others no. Someone I once knew took a few.

ZINNIA: Who's that?

OLIVER: Someone from my past.

ZINNIA: Ex-girlfriend?

OLIVER: (*Pause.*) Not sure that's what you would call it. We were close, but it didn't work out. (*He scoops scrambled eggs onto two plates and takes a plate and a bottle of ketchup over to Zinnia.*) Here you are. I'm taking this opportunity to serve you now.

ZINNIA: (*Sitting down on the floor by the record player.*) Do you mind if I put another record on?

OLIVER: (*Going back to the kitchen to get his plate and turn off the appliances.*) After we're done eating, sure.

ZINNIA: (*Searching her purse for her cell phone.*) I've almost forgotten to check my phone. This isn't going to be good. (*She's staring at her phone.*) Four missed calls. (*Pause.*) I don't recognize any of these numbers. (*Pause.*) Twenty-two texts ... (*Pause.*) ... I'll read those later.

OLIVER: (*Sitting down on the corner of his bed close to her with his food.*) Your Mom wasn't calling you?

ZINNIA: (*Putting ketchup on her eggs.*) No, she thinks I'm with Holly.

OLIVER: Why would she think that?

ZINNIA: (*Hesitant.*) I talked to her and Dad earlier in the evening and I told them that.

OLIVER: You ... hold on. You told me you didn't have a ride last night.

ZINNIA: I didn't.

OLIVER: Holly was supposed to be your ride.

ZINNIA: That got cancelled, she had to do some family thing.

OLIVER: But you didn't say that.

ZINNIA: I'm sorry if I didn't keep you up to date on everything that was going on. You didn't tell me your friend cancelled for dinner.

OLIVER: I didn't think it mattered. So what did you tell Holly?

ZINNIA: (*Suddenly annoyed.*) I don't know. I can't remember everything I tell to everybody at all times, okay?

OLIVER: (*Smiling.*) All right, I'm sorry.

(*He starts laughing a little to himself.*)

ZINNIA: (*Uncomfortable.*) What? What's funny?

OLIVER: Nothing, just ... nothing.

ZINNIA: What, were you thinking of some other conversation with some other girl you lured into here?

OLIVER: (*Stunned.*) Whoa, stop there. I don't "lure" people here like some predator. That's not me. At all.

ZINNIA: There are rumors.

OLIVER: What rumors?

ZINNIA: Things that have gone around. Come on, you never got wind of any of them?

OLIVER: You're making this up, just stop. Do you like your eggs?

ZINNIA: Two years ago. (*Pause.*) Celia? Ring a bell?

OLIVER: Celia ... (*Thinking.*) ... You mean Celia Taylor?

ZINNIA: That's the one.

OLIVER: There are rumors about me and Celia? That's ... come on.

ZINNIA: At the time I didn't believe it. But now, maybe there's something to it?

OLIVER: You're just being mean. Nothing happened between her and I.

ZINNIA: She was always prowling around you. (*Pause.*) Other people noticed.

OLIVER: I ... come on. Just because someone talks to me doesn't mean anything. That's, in a sense, what I'm supposed to do. Talk. That's what I get paid to do.

ZINNIA: You talked to me. I was always in front of the room based on your seating chart.

OLIVER: (*Annoyed.*) The seating chart was alphabetical. (*Setting down his plate.*) What's going on? I made you breakfast, I have coffee here. I'm trying to be ... a good host. (*Pause.*) This was a mistake. I should take you home.

ZINNIA: You're able to drive?

OLIVER: After I finish these eggs up and drink some more water I'll be able to drive.

(*The two sit quietly for a while, both forcing down their food.*)

ZINNIA: So Celia was never in here?

OLIVER: Not once, not ever.

(*They go back to being quiet.*)

ZINNIA: When I was five or six my Mom bought me a watercolor set for Christmas along with some Canson paper. She used to see me drawing all over the bills and paperwork she had around the table and thought to encourage me at the time but she later came to regret it. I started drawing on the driveway with chalk in the summer and made these really elaborate landscapes and I wouldn't let my Dad park on it until the rain started. If we went on vacation, I used to beg to go to at least one art museum nearby. Saw the San Diego Museum of Art and the MoCA in Los Angeles that way. Oh ... and the Getty Museum, which was like walking through a castle filled with lost dreams. But we don't have the money to go a lot of places, so I've been limited in that way. (*Pause.*) Once I got a library card I think I took out every coffee table art book from our lousy, cheap library. I scrounged together tracing paper so I could get a better idea of how the greats mastered composition. (*Pause.*) I've done portraits of every member of my family in oil. I gave them to them as Christmas gifts two years ago. I guess they liked them but no one said. Not one of the paintings ever went up on a wall that I know of. My aunt said she liked hers but that was the last I heard from her about it. (*Pause.*) Sophomore year, I started experimenting with making sculptures out of large, carefully stacked balls of yarn that I had to re-wind myself and attach to metal pieces I salvaged from a scrap yard. I showed them to two girls I thought were my friends and they went "oh, okay" and then later on I heard the one say that it looked "tacky" and "cheap" which hurt. It hurt a lot. (*Pause.*) I have stolen money from almost everyone I know to buy paint and brushes and canvases since I got tired of asking for it every week and I didn't have a job. On my computer I have a Microsoft Excel document that lists how much I owe each person for taking the money from them. I plan, once I get established, to mail everyone a check covering what I owe and then some. This thought helps me sleep better. Well, that and the Lunesta. (*Pause.*) Other people graduated in June and have a good idea of what they want to do and here I am reaching far for something impractical. More than one person in school said I was a "dirty hippie," whatever that's supposed to mean. (*Pause.*) The few knowledgeable people in the field that I've talked to keep saying *experience, experience, you need to gain experience* and let it work through you. (*Pause.*) *You have to treat success and failure as the same thing,* one artist I talked to told me. (*Pause.*) Painting is the only thing I know how to do besides wait tables. I almost flunked chemistry but was lucky I was in a class with idiots. Didn't do a whole lot better in bio or even earth science. (*Pause.*) It's terrifying to think of what I'm supposed to do in life if I can only make a living going into and out of kitchens.

(*The room is quiet for a little bit.*)

OLIVER: (*Nodding.*) I hear you. But you might be getting anxious without knowing where life is going to take you. Jumping the gun, as it were. (*Pause.*) For what it's worth, I think you're a fine writer, too. You did an excellent job with some of the short stories and essays you had to read and interpret.

ZINNIA: Like "The Hunger Artist"? (*Pause.*) I felt like you assigned that because of me.

OLIVER: No, I cover that every year. Without fail. I always like the interpretations I get of it, even from those who skim read it or just do an Internet search.

(*The room is quiet again.*)

ZINNIA: I need to wash up. Is that all right?

OLIVER: Sure, no problem. There's a large stack of towels in there and some wash rags. There should be some shampoo, too.

ZINNIA: (*Getting up and taking some of her clothes with her, including her cell phone.*) Thanks. I won't be long.

OLIVER: Take as long as you need. (*Zinnia goes into the bathroom. In a few moments he hears the shower get turned on. Oliver goes over to the end table by the bed and looks at his cell phone.*) Five missed calls? (*He presses some buttons and places the phone next to his ear. He then taps some more and puts it to his ear again and listens. Pause.*) Damn it. (*He checks to make sure the shower is still running, moves downstage, dials a number and waits a few seconds.*) Good ... it's his voice mail. (*Pause.*) Andrew, it's me, it's early. Sorry, I was going to call you yesterday to tell you I couldn't make it but my phone was dying and for some reason had no reception. I had to drop something off for my Dad and then got caught in traffic and things got really hectic around here. By the time I got back to my place it was late and I was exhausted and thought I'd wait til morning to call back when my phone was charged. So, again, sorry about that. We should reschedule something, I promise I'll be there. (*Laughs.*) Call or text me, whatever's best. Bye. (*He hangs up.*)

(*Oliver goes to the refrigerator and sneaks out a beer from the back, cracks it open and takes a long swig before putting it back inside. He walks over to his bed, takes off his towel, puts on a pair of shorts and a T-shirt and examines the back wall filled with framed pictures. After much deliberation, he stands on the bed and removes several photos and prints until there is a large empty space in the middle directly above the bed. He crawls back down and looks at the wall once more. He then stacks the removed frames next to the bed. The shower stops running. Oliver goes over to the record player and looks through his own collection. The sky is a little brighter orange than before.*)

OLIVER: (*Walking over to the bathroom door and knocking.*) Do you like classical music? (*He doesn't get a response.*) Zin? Classical? (*She still doesn't respond.*) Do you like classical music? Pianos and strings and all that fancy stuff?

ZINNIA: (*Behind the door.*) Sure, whatever you want. I'm almost done.

OLIVER: What about krautrock?

ZINNIA: I don't care. What's krautrock?

OLIVER: Germans. On drugs. With synthesizers.

ZINNIA: Put on whatever.

OLIVER: Will do.

(*He goes back over to the record collection and sorts through them for a little bit, checking the sleeves and then putting them back. Zinnia comes out of the bathroom with the same polo shirt on but wearing a pair of jeans and shoes. Her hair is still a little wet.*)

ZINNIA: You have a really nice bathroom. The steam in the one in my house has no way of ventilating because I think the fan is busted so it turns into a sauna and you can barely see your hand in front of your face. (*Pause.*) What, no music?

OLIVER: I decided to wait for you to choose. I've heard all of these many, many times, so I want you to pick.

ZINNIA: I don't know. Something mellow, maybe?

OLIVER: Pick one.

ZINNIA: (*Looking through the collection.*) What about this? (*She hands him a record.*)

OLIVER: Good choice, good choice. (*He puts it on.*) Ordered this from an online record store in Canada. (*Pause.*)

I want to show you something. Look. (*He points to the back wall.*)

ZINNIA: You took down a lot of your photos! Why?

OLIVER: That space is for you.

ZINNIA: (*Taken aback.*) What do you mean?

OLIVER: You said you made paintings for your entire family and they never hung them up. I made space for you. No obligation. But if you want to give me something, it goes up there.

ZINNIA: I ... I'm not sure I have anything right now....

OLIVER: It doesn't have to be at this moment. Think of it like a reserved parking space with your name on it.

(*Zinnia goes over to the stack of frames Oliver took off the wall and looks through them.*)

ZINNIA: But you took down some of your best pictures. (*Pause.*) Like this one of you. Where's this from?

OLIVER: That's me in front of The Atomium in Brussels.

ZINNIA: Was it digitally edited?

OLIVER: No. The person that took it used a Pentax K1000 using Ilford 400 film pushed to 800. I don't know much about photography but I do remember that. She developed the print herself.

ZINNIA: It has an eerie quality about it. Kind of ... stark. (*She examines another framed photo.*) What about this one?

OLIVER: (*Pause.*) There I'm in front of the St. Vitus Cathedral in Prague. Funny story about that one ... or, maybe it's not that funny. So me and this person I'm with—

ZINNIA: (*Interrupting.*) Does this person have a name?

OLIVER: Yes, but it's not important. We're having lunch sort of close to the Astronomical Clock. We get sausages, cabbage, potatoes ... it's a heavy meal. So we see on the menu they have absinthe—

ZINNIA: (*Interrupting.*) "The Green Fairy." It doesn't really affect you the way it's rumored to. I've read a lot about it.

OLIVER: Right, well, we tried taking that to the extreme. (*Pause.*) Mind if I turn off the record player? (*He goes over and turns it off.*) So, I ordered one drink after another after another, and she was edging me on a little, you know? I just washed them down. Had to have been at least four. I figured the weight of the food would absorb some of it? It did not. So we finish eating and I'm wobbling around. We make our way across the Charles, we get to Prague Castle, I'm really unsteady. She wants one photo of just me in front of it. That is the only good picture that came out of it. The rest I'm either leaning or standing awkwardly. (*Laughs to himself.*) You had to be there. (*Pause.*) No hallucinations, though. I kept waiting for those to kick in.

ZINNIA: So what happened?

OLIVER: I sobered up back in the hotel room. Kind of ruined the day.

ZINNIA: No, what happened to your relationship with this person.

OLIVER: (*Long Pause.*) We were engaged. (*He goes through the frames.*) Check this out. (*He hands her a photo.*) I took it. I'm with my parents and my brother in Arches National Park. Almost impossible to get a bad picture depending on where you go.

ZINNIA: So she broke off the engagement?

OLIVER: (*Pause.*) I did. She thought she was my mother. Or at least acted like it. (*Pause.*) A lot happened. I shouldn't pretend like it's her fault and she jilted me. And looking back, and we're talking ... five years now ... something like that, I was in the wrong, mostly. The only thing I blame her for is not trying to understand me better. (*Pause.*) That sounds bad, I probably shouldn't say that either. (*Pause.*) You know what they say about problems stacking up? Well, my best friend from childhood who moved away is getting married. In two weeks. (*Pause.*) I'm supposed to drive down to Charleston for it. And I don't want to go.

ZINNIA: (*She sets down the photo.*) Why not? You have to go.

OLIVER: I don't know.

ZINNIA: You're being a child. Your friend expects you.

OLIVER: I know ... I realize that. I've been trying to coax my brother into going down with me. But he's been dodging it. "Work commitments" ... I keep hearing that. He already has one vacation planned for the middle of August and "can't take more time off."

ZINNIA: You might have a fun time just by yourself.

OLIVER: Like I said before, I'm not the most ... open person. I also feel like he's doing what I should be doing. (*Pause.*) But I don't need to go over all that. Say, it's a nice day out, we're both dressed. (*Goes and pours himself more coffee.*) How about we go for a walk? Spend the day together, get lunch.

ZINNIA: I work tonight, so I should get home and rest up.

OLIVER: We could just hang out in here. I can pick us up something to eat later and then you can go right to work from here.

ZINNIA: Actually, my boyfriend's going to be picking me up in a couple of minutes.

OLIVER: (*Stunned.*) Boyfriend? You have a boyfriend?

ZINNIA: (*Confused.*) I'm pretty sure you know who Paul is. We went to the prom together. (*Oliver doesn't say anything.*) You were one of the school's chauffeurs, don't act like you didn't see the two of us.

OLIVER: Not all "prom dates" are couples. Sometimes two people just go together ... just to go. I've seen it happen before.

ZINNIA: We've been together since the start of Senior Year.

OLIVER: (*Staring.*) How ... how do you explain ... this, then?

ZINNIA: What do you mean?

OLIVER: I'm pretty certain that what went between you and me constitutes cheating.

ZINNIA: I wouldn't say that.

OLIVER: That's ... exactly what happened.

ZINNIA: I don't look at it like that. I have very strong feelings for Paul. He's going to school in New Brunswick, I'm going to be in Manhattan. We're going to be able to see each other often.

OLIVER: How do you think he'd feel if he knew you were with another person?

ZINNIA: I don't know.

OLIVER: How would you feel if he was with another person?

ZINNIA: Paul? (*Laughs.*) He was just having a game night with his friends.

OLIVER: But how do you know he wasn't with anyone and just telling you that?

ZINNIA: Not a chance.

OLIVER: So ... is he picking you up ... here?

ZINNIA: Yes. I said to find an empty space if he could and I'd meet him outside.

OLIVER: (*Starting to pace around.*) What did you tell him you're doing here?

ZINNIA: I texted him in the bathroom to see if he was awake, and he was, and then asked if he could pick me up. And he said yeah, I'll be there.

OLIVER: Who did you tell him you were with?

ZINNIA: I said I crashed at a friend's place. He didn't ask for more details.

OLIVER: (*Pause.*) Wait, wait, wait ... why wasn't he able to pick you up last night? He couldn't take a "break" from hanging out? And then you said you were supposed to go with Holly? I'm a little confused.

ZINNIA: You know what, you're asking way too many questions.

OLIVER: You don't think this is a little bit ... not normal?

ZINNIA: I'm not sure what I would call it. (*Pause.*) What did you call what happened with Celia Taylor?

OLIVER: I wouldn't call that anything because nothing happened between us, which I said before. (*Pause.*) How much is enough with you?

(*Zinnia checks her phone.*)

ZINNIA: Paul's close by. I need to go. (*She moves towards the exit.*)

OLIVER: Wait, wait, wait. Can you please just tell me what's going on. Was it something I said? It can't be over some rumor that for some reason you didn't mention at all last night but can't stop going on about now.

ZINNIA: I'm not sure what's happening, only that I should leave.

OLIVER: All right. That's fine. I hope you have all your things.

ZINNIA: I do. (*Pause.*) Please go to your friend's wedding. That's all I ask.

OLIVER: (*Hesitantly.*) I will.

ZINNIA: It will do you good.

(*She opens the door and exits. Oliver stands by the doorway and talks to her before she gets into the unseen elevator.*)

OLIVER: You're not mad at me, right? I don't want to leave this with you upset in any way. (*Pause.*) If you want to send me artwork ... or drop it off ... I was serious about that. (*The elevator dings. Oliver waits a moment, receives no response and then closes the door behind him. He opens up the fridge and takes out the opened beer and drinks some before setting it down on the counter. He picks up her plate of food and coffee mug and looks out the bay window to the street below.*) I'll be damned, that is Paul. (*After a long pause, he hears two car doors shut, one a few seconds after the other.*) I wonder if she realizes she's still wearing my shirt.

CURTAIN.

www.ingramcontent.com/pod-product-compliance
Lightning Source LLC
Chambersburg PA
CBHW070642130626
46555CB00006B/2664